Nugget & Darling

By Barbara M. Joosse

Illustrated by Sue Truesdell

CLARION BOOKS/New York

Clarion Books
a Houghton Mifflin Company imprint
215 Park Avenue South, New York, NY 10003
Text copyright © 1997 by Barbara M. Joosse
Illustrations copyright © 1997 by Sue Truesdell

The illustrations were executed in pen and ink with watercolor on Arches.
The text was set in 17-point Novarese.

www.houghtonmifflinbooks.com

Printed in Singapore.

Library of Congress Cataloging-in-Publication Data

Joosse, Barbara M.
Nugget and Darling / by Barbara M. Joosse ; illustrated by Sue Truesdell
p.   cm.
Summary: Nell has to deal with her dog Nugget's reaction when a kitten appears on the scene.
ISBN 0-395-64571-9   PA ISBN 0-618-11141-7
[1. Dogs—Fiction. 2. Cats—Fiction. 3. Jealousy—Fiction.]
I. Truesdell, Sue, ill. II. Title.
PZ7.J7435Nu   1997
[E]—dc20   94-17011
CIP
AC

TWP   10   9   8   7   6   5

For Charley,
thank you for making art.
—B.M.J.

For Barbara Dicks.
—S.T.

When Nell was cold,
Nugget kept her feet warm.
When she was sad,
Nugget pretended he was a jack-in-the-box.

Sometimes they did magic tricks.
Nell wore a swirly purple cape
and waved a sparkly wand.
Nugget wore rabbit ears.
Their favorite trick was Magic Cups.

"The hand is quicker than the eye," Nell said.
She put a ball under one cup
and swiveled the cups around.
She tried to fool Nugget. "Pick a cup, any cup."
But Nugget knew which cup to choose.

When it was time for bed,
Nugget licked Nell with his soft, pink tongue.
Nell tickled Nugget behind his ears,
the secret place Nugget liked best.
Then Nugget lay down beside Nell,
on the rug that was the color of his fur.
Ahhh.

One day, Nugget heard a small noise.
He swept his nose back and forth, searching.
What was it?
Nugget poked under the leaves and sniffed.
A *kitten!* A *tiny wet kitten!*

Nugget grabbed Nell's pants with his teeth and pulled.
Come on!

He raced ahead.
Hurry!

"Look at the little darling!" Nell cried. "She's shivering."
Nell wrapped her sweater around the kitten and took
her home.

Nell lined a basket with a dry washcloth
and placed the kitten inside.
"I'm going to call you Darling."
Nell's voice was soft and fuzzy,
the way it was when she talked to Nugget.

Nell warmed some milk and gave it to Darling.
Nugget pushed his nose into Darling's basket.
What about me?
"Nugget!" Nell scolded. "Don't drink that milk.
It's for Darling!"
Nugget knew that.

That night, Nell tied a floppy bow
on the handle of Darling's basket
and set it on the golden rug beside her bed.
Nugget's rug!
"You can sleep right next to Nugget," she told Darling.
"You don't mind, do you, Nugget?"

But Nugget *did* mind.
The rug smelled like him and had his hair on it.
And that was the way he liked it.

Nugget found a spot next to the window,
away from Darling.
He spun around in a tight circle
and flopped on the floor.
H*mmmf*.

The floor was hard and far from Nell,
but at least it wasn't close to Darling.

Nell missed Nugget beside her.
"Come, Nugget," she said, patting his rug.
But Nugget stayed where he was.

Most mornings,
Nell and Nugget went to the tree house.
Nugget guarded the bottom
while Nell told him jokes from the top.
That was what they *always* did.
Now Nell took Darling into the cool branches.

Me, too! Me, too! barked Nugget,
jumping against the tree.
Then he ran around the tree a few times
before he slumped underneath.

Nell told Nugget a joke
about a green, slimy thing running up her arm.
But she was holding Darling,
and it wasn't the same.

19

That afternoon, Nell performed magic tricks
for Nugget and Darling. Darling wore a tiny cape.
Nell set out the magic cups.
"The hand is quicker than the eye," she said.

Nugget couldn't see!
He stood on his hind legs
and rested his paws on the table
to get a better look.

Wham!
The table crashed to the floor.
Darling flew in the air, cape and all.
Mrraaaiw!

Nell picked up Darling and cradled her in her arms.
"Nugget!" she scolded. "You frightened Darling!"

Nugget didn't mean to scare Darling.
He just wanted to see where Nell had put the ball.
But Nell looked angry.
Nugget's tail drooped between his legs
and he slunk away.

"Nugget!" Nell called, but Nugget didn't turn around.

"I really fussed over Darling," Nell said to herself.
"Nugget must think I don't like him anymore."

Nell had to show Nugget he was wrong.

Gently, she pulled him up from the floor.

"Come outside," she said.
She raced ahead. "Hurry!"

When Nugget saw the bedspread made into a tent,
he sniffed it.
"Nugget!" Nell said. "This is just for you.
See? The sign says,
    NUGGET'S HIDEOUT. NO CATS ALLOWED."

Inside, Nell put on her magic cape
and placed the rabbit ears on Nugget's head.
She set out the cups
and put a ball inside one of them.
"Watch carefully, Nugget," she said.
"The hand is quicker than the eye."

Nell swiveled the cups around.
"Pick a cup, any cup," she said.
Nugget knew which cup to choose.

When it was time for bed,
Nell switched Darling's basket to the other side.
"Darling," she said. "this is your spot now."
Nell put Darling in the basket.
Nugget rolled around on the rug.
It smelled like him and had his hair on it.

He still didn't like Darling very much,
but he liked her better on the other side of the bed.

Nugget walked over to Darling's side
and gave the kitten a lick—
a very tiny lick.
Darling purred.

Nugget went back to his side.
He licked Nell with his soft, pink tongue.
Nell tickled the soft spot beneath Nugget's ears,
the secret place Nugget liked best.
Then Nugget lay down beside Nell,
on the little rug that was the color of his fur.
His rug. *Ahhh.*